DETROIT PUBLIC LIBRARY
9
D0006085

I shook the magic ball. "Magic fortune-telling ball," I said, "will I have fun on my field trip?"

I turned the ball over and read the message.

"CONCENTRATE AND ASK AGAIN," it said.

I tried again. "Will I have fun at the apple orchard?"

"ABSOLUTELY, POSITIVELY YES!" it said.

Of course, I already knew that would be the answer.

KNAPP BRANCH LIBRARY
13330 CONANT
DETROIT, MICHIGAN 48212
(313) 481-1772
KN
SEP 12

Never Swim in Applesauce

The Roscoe Riley Rules books
by Katherine Applegate

Roscoe Riley Rules #1:
Never Glue Your Friends to Chairs

Roscoe Riley Rules #2:
Never Swipe a Bully's Bear

Roscoe Riley Rules #3:
Don't Swap Your Sweater for a Dog

Roscoe Riley Rules #4:
Never Swim in Applesauce

ROSCOE RILEY RULES

#4

Never Swim in Applesauce

Katherine Applegate
illustrated by Brian Biggs

HarperTrophy®
An Imprint of HarperCollins*Publishers*

Harper Trophy® is a registered trademark of
HarperCollins Publishers
Roscoe Riley Rules #4: Never Swim
in Applesauce
Text copyright © 2008 by Katherine Applegate
Illustrations copyright © 2008 by Brian Biggs
All rights reserved.
Printed in the United States of America. No part of
this book may be used or reproduced in any manner
whatsoever without written permission except in the
case of brief quotations embodied in critical articles
and reviews.
For information address HarperCollins
Children's Books, a division of HarperCollins Publishers,
10 East 53rd Street, New York, NY 10022.
www.harpercollinschildrens.com

Library of Congress Cataloging-in-Publication Data
is available.
ISBN 978-0-06-114887-3 (pbk.)
ISBN 978-0-06-114888-0 (trade bdg.)

11 12 13 LP/CW 10 9 8 7

❖

First Edition

This book is for Austin
from his friends
Katherine and Goofy

Contents

#4 Never Swim in Applesauce

1

Welcome to Time-Out

Yep. It's me. Roscoe Riley.

Stuck in time-out again.

And speaking of stuck, have I got a story for you!

A very sticky story.

See, my class went on a field trip to an apple farm.

A field trip is when you go somewhere

more fun than even recess and lunch put together.

We went to an apple farm so we could learn about where our food comes from.

Besides the pizza delivery guy.

All the kids went. And our teacher.

And some moms and dads to make sure we didn't get rowdy or do trouble-making.

I didn't get rowdy.

Well, maybe just once or twice.

But I *did* get into a teeny, tiny, practically invisible bit of trouble.

Who knew there was a rule about not jumping into a giant tub of applesauce?

I'll bet you've done some applesauce swimming, haven't you?

No?

Well, trust me on this. You should stick

to swimming in real, live swimming pools.

Applesauce is very . . . well, appley.

But maybe I should start at the beginning.

The part before I got apple-slimed.

2

Something You Should Know Before We Get Started

Worms are good for fishing and for scaring little sisters and sometimes dads.

But they do not make a very good snack.

I hear they taste sort of like mushy macaroni.

3

Something Else You Should Know Before We Get Started

Everybody loves plain applesauce.

And cinnamon applesauce.

And even raspberry-flavored applesauce.

But boy-flavored applesauce?

Not so much.

4

Happy Apple Orchard

When I first heard about our field trip, I was pretty excited.

Almost as excited as my teacher, Ms. Diz.

She told us about the trip in a very thrilled way, with tons of exclamation points in her voice.

"Children!" Ms. Diz said first thing that morning. "I have a wonderful surprise! This

Friday we are going on a field trip! The first one for our class!" She grinned. "And the first one for me since I became a teacher!"

Ms. Diz is a brand-new teacher. I help her out whenever I can.

I know a lot because I am a retired kindergartner.

"My brother's class went on a trip to a bakery and they got free doughnuts," I said.

Then I raised my hand real quick because sometimes I forget to remember that part.

You aren't supposed to talk until you put your hand up in the air and wave it like crazy because that is better than just yelling at the top of your lungs.

"If we can't go on a bakery field trip, maybe a cotton-candy factory would be good. Or an aquarium with giant, kid-eating sharks," I added.

Sometimes my imagination button gets stuck on fast-forward.

"Those are great suggestions, Roscoe," said Ms. Diz. "But we've already made plans for this trip. I'll give you a hint, class. What have we been learning about the past few weeks?"

"If you squeeze your juice box hard, you get a gusher!" said Dewan.

"Do not pick your nose during snack time," Coco said.

For some reason, she looked right at me.

"The pencil sharpener is not for crayons," Gus offered.

Ms. Diz held up her hands to make a *T*. Like a coach taking a time-out.

She does that when she wants us to be

quiet. Which is pretty often, come to think of it.

"We've been learning about *where our food comes from*," Ms. Diz reminded us.

She said the last part very slowly. So our brains could catch up with her mouth.

"Remember we talked about how vegetables and fruits come from farms?" Ms. Diz asked. "And about how the farmers grow the food and pick it, then send it on trucks to stores where we can buy it? I know how much you guys love applesauce, and apple pies, and taffy apples," Ms. Diz said. "That's why we are going to visit—"

I finished for her. "THE GROCERY STORE!!!" I yelled. "I LOVE the grocery store because I push the cart for my mom and dad except not anymore because I knocked over a watermelon pile and that knocked over a lemon pile and whoa, that was cool because it looked just like pink lemonade!"

"Roscoe," said Ms. Diz while I stopped

to take a breath, "I need you to think before speaking. Okay?"

I thought for a while. "Okay!" I said after I figured I'd been thinking long enough.

"As I was trying to say," said Ms. Diz, "we are going to an apple orchard!"

"You mean where they make apples?" Gus asked.

"They don't *make* apples, they *grow* them," said Ms. Diz. "There are hundreds of apple trees at Happy Apple Orchard. They produce all kinds of apples. Green and red and yellow, sweet and sour. We'll each get to pick our own apples!"

That was way better than a field trip to a plain old field!

We did a lot of cheering and jumping out of our chairs and clapping.

Until Ms. Diz had to ring her gong.

It is a very loud bell that helps us Stay Focused.

Staying Focused is when you Stop Acting Like Preschoolers, Class.

"They make lots of food at Happy Apple too," Ms. Diz said when we were quiet. "We'll get to see them bake apple pies and make applesauce. We might even get to *eat* some! But only if you all are on your best behavior."

Pie and applesauce? That was too much great news.

Ms. Diz had to gong four times before we settled down.

But who could blame us?

We were going on a field trip to see happy apples!

5

The Magic Fortune-Telling Ball

When my brother, Max, and I got home from school that afternoon, my dad was in the kitchen.

Some days Dad works at home.

He says it makes him appreciate the office more.

"Dad!" I yelled. "We are going on a field

trip! My whole class!"

"Get a chocolate doughnut when you go," Max said. "The jelly ones are stale."

"We aren't going to a bakery," I said. "We are going to an apple maker."

"You mean an orchard?" Dad said. "Cool."

Max made a face. "Better luck next time."

"Sounds like fun to me," said Dad. "Roscoe will get to pick apples, I'll bet. And who knows? Maybe they'll have free taffy apples. Or free pie." He got a big smile on his face. "I do love a good apple pie. Especially a free one."

My little sister, Hazel, came into the kitchen. She was wearing a black pirate eye patch, overalls, a fluffy pink ballet tutu, and a pair of my dad's old sneakers.

"Hazel, my dear, as always you are looking very fashionable," Dad said.

If you ask me, little kids should not be allowed to dress themselves.

"Did somebody say *pie*?" Hazel asked.

"I'm going on a field trip to an apple-growing place," I explained. "They might even give away pie and applesauce."

"Applesauce is my favorite," Hazel said. "Except for gummi worms and broccoli."

Hazel pulled a small red ball out of one of her pockets.

Hazel loved that ball. She carried it everywhere she went. And she refused to share it.

Of course, it wasn't just a plain old everyday ball. It was a magic ball that could tell the future.

All you had to do was shake it. Then

ask it a yes-or-no kind of question.

When you turned it over, there on the bottom, in a little bitty window, was your answer.

Hazel can't read yet. I think she just liked the ball because it was so shiny.

And because Max and I wanted to play with it.

"Magic ball, will I ever get to go on a field trip and eat pie?" Hazel asked.

She turned the ball over. "What does it say?" she asked Dad.

Dad looked at the bottom of the ball. "It says, 'YOU BETTER BELIEVE IT!'"

"Can I borrow your ball for one second?" I asked Hazel. "I just want to ask it about my field trip."

"Nope." Hazel shook her head.

"*Please?*" I begged. I smiled my best smile.

The one that makes Grandma say, "You old charmer, you!"

It works on grandmas.

But not so much on little sisters.

Hazel shook her head again. "Nope."

She tossed her ball in the air. When

she tried to catch it in her tutu, the ball dropped onto the floor.

It rolled behind the refrigerator.

"I'll get it for you, Hazel," Max said.

"No, wait! I'll get it!" I said quickly.

Because I am a helpful brother.

And also because I really wanted to get my hands on that ball.

"I have dibs," Max said.

"You just want it 'cause I want it," I said to Max.

"You just want it 'cause Hazel says you can't have it," Max replied.

It was hard to argue with that one.

"Besides," Max added, "you had a ball like that and you lost it."

"I didn't lose it," I said. "I accidentally dropped it in the garbage disposal when I was giving it a bath."

"We paid three hundred and twenty dollars to repair the disposal, if I recall correctly," said Dad.

"I don't want to get my tutu dirty," Hazel said. "Whoever gets the ball can play with it."

Max and I dashed to the refrigerator.

He took one side. I took the other.

We both reached for the ball.

I had to lie on the floor and s-t-r-e-t-c-h my left arm extra far.

When I stood up, I had dog hair, dust balls, and three Froot Loops stuck to my shirt. But I also had the ball.

I brushed off the hair and dust and ate the Froot Loops.

"Roscoe," Dad said, "please save the floor food for the dog. And why are you two so interested in that ball?"

"It's not just a ball, Dad," I said. "It's a ball that tells the future."

"I got it at Howie Hubble's birthday party," Hazel said. "'Cause I won pin-the-tail-on-the-donkey."

She started to take the ball from my hand.

"C'mon, Hazel," I begged. "You said whoever rescued the ball could play with it."

"You have got to promise, promise, PROMISE to give this back to me. Soon," Hazel said.

"How about Friday?" I asked.

"Promise?"

"I promise," I said. "You can count on me."

"Cross your heart and hope to fry?"

"Trust me, Hazel," I said.

"I trusted you with my Butterfly Barbie, and you let the dog eat one of her wings."

"That was a total accident. I wanted to see if she could fly," I explained. "And Goofy thought she was a Frisbee. I promise you that nothing will happen to this ball."

"Okay," she said, but she sounded like she didn't believe me.

I shook the magic ball. "Magic fortune-telling ball," I said, "will I have fun on my field trip?"

I turned the ball over and read the message.

"CONCENTRATE AND ASK AGAIN," it said.

I tried again. "Will I have fun at the apple orchard?"

"ABSOLUTELY, POSITIVELY YES!" it said.

Of course, I already knew that would be the answer.

6

One Hundred Apples Up High in a Tree

When our field-trip day finally came, I woke up extra early to be sure I wouldn't miss anything.

Turns out four in the morning is a little *too* early.

Moms and dads are very grumbly that time of day.

After I took the bus to school, we did the usual morning stuff.

The Pledge of a Wee Gent.

Morning Nouncements.

Calendar.

Weather.

And Sharing Time.

I shared Hazel's magic fortune-telling ball.

It was my second time sharing it.

But Ms. Diz said that was okay because I was clearly very attached to it.

Also, it was my last day of having the ball.

After school I had to give it back to Hazel.

She'd reminded me at breakfast.

Twice.

The first time I shared the ball, I had forgotten to ask it a yes-or-no question.

This time I asked it, "Will this be my

most funnest day ever?"

I turned it over and checked the answer.

"'OUTLOOK CLOUDY,'" I read.

"It's going to rain?" Gus cried. "But that means no apple picking!"

"I think the ball means a different kind of cloudy," said Ms. Diz. "It means it's not sure what the answer is. But let's remember it's just a toy, and toys can't tell the future.

Besides, I think it's a pretty safe bet that today will be a fun day for all of you."

At last we lined up and headed outside to the field-trip bus.

I sat next to Emma. She's my best friend.

Gus sat in front of us. He's my other best friend.

Gus had to sit next to Wyatt.

Sometimes I call Wyatt "Bully Breath."

When I do that, Mom corrects me. "Let's just say that Wyatt does not exactly have a winning personality," she says.

But that's way too many words to remember.

Today we had to be polite to Wyatt because he was part of our apple-picking team.

On the bus there were some moms and dads, but my mom and dad couldn't come because they had to work.

Which was okay. Because sometimes parents can be embarrassing.

Like when they wipe your nose with a tissue when you have a perfectly good sleeve available.

Before we got going, Ms. Diz stood up at the front of the bus.

We were pretty exuberant.

Emma taught me that word. She likes words a lot.

It means "full of excitement."

Only *exuberant* sounds better.

We were so exuberant, I'll bet Ms. Diz wished she had her gong with her.

"I know you're all thrilled about our first field trip!" said Ms. Diz when we finally quieted down. "Now, when we first arrive at the orchard, we are going to listen to a lecture. After that we will pick apples. Do you all remember the rule we talked about?"

"Stay with your apple team!" we yelled.

"This is our very first field trip," Ms. Diz said. "So *please* let's be on our best behavior, okay, kids? No trouble, or we won't be able to have another trip someday."

The bus engine roared. We waved

good-bye to our school.

"Happy apples, here we come!" I said.

All the way to the apple farm we sang a fun song.

It is called "One Hundred Apples Up High in a Tree."

Here is how it goes. In case you ever drive to an apple farm and need some entertainment.

One hundred apples up high in a tree!
One hundred apples up high!
Take one down and pass it around.
Ninety-nine apples up high in a tree!

Then you sing "Ninety-nine apples up high in a tree."

Then ninety-eight.

Then ninety-seven.

You keep on going until you get to "One apple up high in a tree."

And then—bam! You start all over again.

We sang that song a zillion times.

And nobody ever got tired of it.

Except I think maybe Coco's mom didn't like it so much.

On account of she put Kleenex in her ears.

7

Granny Smiths

Happy Apple Orchard had rows and rows of apple trees.

And a tour guy to show us how to pick apples. He had a green shirt with a red apple on the pocket.

His name was Abe.

Abe said apples are good for you. So it's not even cheating that they taste good too.

Abe showed us how the inside of the

apple has little black seeds in it.

Whole entire trees grow up from them!

Abe told us that the fuzzy part at the bottom of an apple is called a sepal.

He also said most of an apple is made of water, but there's some air in there too.

That's why apples float!

Finally the learning part was over and it was time to PICK!

Abe gave each team a big basket to carry their apples in.

"Now, here's what we're going to do," he said. "Each apple team will get their own tree. You may pick as many apples as you like, until your arms get tired or your basket is full. Whichever comes first."

Each of our apple teams had four people. And each team was named after a kind of apple.

There was a Golden Delicious Team.

And a Gala Team.

And a McIntosh Team.

We were the Granny Smith Team.

Granny Smith is the name of a sourish green apple.

It is probably the name of somebody's grandma too.

"These baskets hold a lot of apples, my friends. Do you think you will be able to pick that

many?" Abe asked.

I pulled Hazel's magic fortune-telling ball out of my jeans pocket.

"Magic ball, will the Granny Smiths pick a whole basket of apples?" I asked.

I turned it over.

"It says 'NO WAY,'" I said.

"I'll bet you can do it," Abe said. "Especially with the help of a picking pole."

Abe passed each of us a long pole.

At the end of each pole was a little net.

Like a basketball net. Only closed up at the bottom.

"These are picking poles," said Abe. "Think of them as your apple catchers."

"And be very careful with them," Ms. Diz added.

"Now follow me, pickers!" Abe said.

He led us down a trail past lines of apple trees.

He stopped and pointed to a big tree. It had a zillion branches sticking out like big brown arms.

"Granny Smiths, you're first up," he said. "Meet your tree! These are called winesap apples."

It was cool and shadowy under the branches.

Red apples hung down everywhere.

Some were even on the ground.

"Don't eat the ones that have fallen," Abe warned. "They might be rotten. And don't eat the ones you pick from the trees until they've been washed."

Abe borrowed my picking pole and held it up high.

He tapped an apple. It plopped into the little net.

He lowered the stick and held up the apple.

"See?" he said. "That's how you do it. Easy as apple pie."

Abe looked more closely at the apple. "Oops. This one's a dud."

He tossed the apple over his shoulder. "There's a worm in that one. If you see an apple with a hole in it, there might be a worm inside."

The class made lots of *ewww!* noises.

"Okay, Granny Smiths," Abe said, "get to work. I'm going to take the other teams to their trees."

Let me tell you something. Those apples don't exactly *want* to get picked!

They must be pretty happy just hanging there like shiny decorations.

Because some of them hold on awfully tight.

After a while I figured out how to tap

hard with my apple picker.

An apple fell right in!

I pulled down my stick. There in my net was a bright red apple.

It even had a tiny green leaf on the stem.

I put it in our basket.

Emma and Gus and Wyatt each put an apple in too.

"My apple's bigger than your puny one," Wyatt said to me.

I decided to ignore him.

That's usually the best way to deal with Wyatt.

"We'll have a full basket in no time!" Emma said.

I gathered more apples.

One. Two. Three. Four.

It's a whole lot easier just to buy one of those bags of apples at the grocery store.

I was on apple number ten when I heard Wyatt yell, "Look at this sucker!"

He held a great big apple in front of my face.

It was awfully big, I had to admit.

But then I saw an even better apple.

Way up high.

The biggest, shiniest, most juiciest apple in Happy Apple Orchard!

8

The Amazing Apple

I took a swing at that humongous apple and missed by a mile.

Then Wyatt saw it too.

"It's the hugest apple on the planet!" Wyatt cried.

"It's *my* apple!" I said.

"Not if I'm the one who picks it!" he said.

We both swung our sticks at that

gigantic apple.

And we both missed.

We swung again.

Crack! Our sticks hit with a loud whack.

"Boys," Ms. Diz warned, "careful with the sticks!"

"It's just one apple, you know," Emma said. "There are hundreds of apples on this tree."

"It's a super apple!" I corrected.

"It's Gigantor, the Killer Apple from Outer Space!" Wyatt added.

"Wow," Gus said. "It looks like a basket-ball!"

I swung and missed again.

"Guys," Emma said, "our basket is only half full. Everybody else has a ton of ap-ples."

"But they don't have the Awesome, Amazing Super Apple!" Wyatt said.

He swung again and missed.

I had an idea.

"Gus," I said. "Come here. It's time for a ladder."

"We don't have a ladder," Gus pointed out.

"I'll be the ladder," I said.

I got down on my hands and knees.

"Oh." Gus grinned. "I get it."

Gus climbed up on my back. He used his stick for balance.

"Ow," I said. "Ow, ow, ow. Hurry, Gus. Your ladder can't take much more of this."

Whack! Whack! Whack!

Gus kept missing. "Keep still. It's hard to balance when your ladder keeps breathing," he complained.

"Hey, it's cheating if you have to step on a friend," Wyatt said.

"I don't mind," I said.

Even though Gus was turning out to be way heavier than I'd expected.

"Emma," Wyatt said. "Come here. I need to step on you."

"Excuse me? Emma said. She laughed. "No way, Wyatt."

Wyatt turned to Gus.

"Gus," he said. "We need to work together. Stay on Roscoe. I'll climb on your shoulders and whack that apple down."

"How about I climb on you?" Gus asked.

"How about nobody else climbs on me?" I asked.

"I'm taller than you," Wyatt said to Gus.

Gus nodded. "Can't argue with that."

"Yes you can," said Emma. "And are you three aware that this is dumb?"

"I agree with Emma," I said with a groan. "And my back agrees too."

Just then somebody yelled a cover-your-ears kind of yell."OUCH! I'm hit! Call 9-1-1!"

Emma went to find out what was going on.

"It's just Coco," Emma said when she came back. "An apple fell on her head."

Wyatt glanced over his shoulder.

All the teachers and parents were busy with Coco.

"The coast is clear," said Wyatt. "Stand still, Gus."

Gus stayed on me.

Wyatt climbed on him.

"UGH," I said.

One kid is heavy.

Two kids is *too* heavy.

"I am thinking this is a way not-good idea," I said.

I wobbled.

Gus wobbled.

Wyatt wobbled and whacked.

Whack! Whack!

Plop!

"I GOT IT!" Wyatt yelled.

Just before he fell.

And Gus fell.

On me.

"Ouch," I said.

"YOU ouch? What about ME?" Wyatt said, rubbing his elbow. "I was on top."

"Yeah, but I was on the bottom," I said with a groan.

Ms. Diz ran over.

"Boys, what on earth is going on here?" she asked.

"Check out this apple, Ms. Diz!" Wyatt cried.

He pulled that beauty out of the net.

"Let's eat it!" I said.

"Roscoe Riley!" Ms. Diz said. "The apples have to be washed first."

"It's bigger than a melon," Gus said.

"It's bigger than a Halloween pumpkin," I said.

"It's just an apple!" Emma said.

"No more misbehaving, boys," Ms. Diz warned.

"Sorry," we all said.

"You want to be able to go on other field trips, don't you?" Ms. Diz added.

"I vote for the doughnut place next time," I said.

"We'll see," said Ms. Diz. "It will depend on how much I can trust you to behave."

"Five more minutes of picking!" called Abe.

Which was good news.

My arms were tired. And so was my back.

Plus I was kind of sore from being smushed.

I guess Gus and Wyatt were tired too.

Because they sat on the ground with me while Emma kept picking.

I think maybe she's tougher than us guys.

Thanks to Emma, we got that basket almost filled.

But not quite.

"The magic fortune-telling ball was right!" I said. "We didn't fill our basket. But we did get the giant apple."

"Can I see that ball?" Emma asked.

I took it out of my pocket and handed it to her.

She shook the ball. "Magic ball," Emma said, "who should get to take home most of the apples since she did all the work?"

Emma turned over the ball. She grinned.

"'EMMA SHOULD, BECAUSE THOSE GUYS WERE BUSY FIGHTING LIKE MORONS OVER AN APPLE,'" she read.

I am pretty sure she was just pretending, though.

Because that is for sure not a yes-or-no kind of answer.

9

Why You Should Never Eat an Apple with a Hole in It

Abe led us to a wide, long building.

An apple tree was painted on its front door.

Emma and Gus carried our almost-but-not-quite-full basket.

I carried our picking poles.

Wyatt carried the Amazing Apple.

The building smelled yummy inside.

Like cinnamon applesauce and taffy apples.

We set our baskets by the door. Abe gathered up our poles.

"This is where we clean our apples," he said. "We sort them here too. Some of the apples are too little to sell. We use those to make applesauce."

"Do we get to eat some free applesauce?" I asked.

"You sure do," said Abe. "We make applesauce in the room next to this one."

Abe waved for us to follow him. He paused in front of a big glass window.

On the other side we could see giant pots of gooey appley-looking stuff.

"That's the applesauce mixture after it's

been cooked. It's cooled off, and sugar and cinnamon have been added. Next it will go into containers to be sold," Abe explained.

He led us to a huge tub of bubbly water. It was as big as a wading pool. And as high as my belly button.

Apples floated in the water like little boats.

It looked like we were going to have a giant dunking-for-apples Halloween party.

Next to the tub was another one filled with plain water.

After that came a long moving belt.

It looked just like the conveyor belts at the grocery store checkout line.

This one was covered with apples, though, instead of milk cartons and dog food and toilet paper.

I felt in my pocket. The magic fortune-telling ball was still there, safe and sound.

So far, it had been right about whether this would be a good field trip.

I was *definitely* having fun.

"This tub is where the apples get washed," Abe explained. "Think of it as a big apple bathtub."

"Can I wash my Amazing Apple, Abe?"

Wyatt asked.

"*Our* Amazing Apple," I corrected.

Wyatt held up the apple so Abe could see it.

"Whoa, that *is* a big fella," said Abe.

Ms. Diz said, "Boys, every child will take home a bag of apples. Your moms and dads can wash them when you get home, and then you can eat them."

"Here's an idea," Abe said. "Why don't we run this big ol' apple through the wash? It's so huge, the kids might be able to keep track of it. Go ahead, young man. Throw it in the vat with all the bubbles."

Wyatt tossed the apple into the bubbly tub.

Plop!

It disappeared, then floated to the surface.

"Boys and girls," Abe said, "keep your eye on the apple. First it will be washed in this tub. Then it will move on to be rinsed."

The apple disappeared into a metal tube.

Abe led us to the second huge tub. This one didn't have any bubbles.

"There it is!" Gus cried. "I see it!"

Everyone cheered for the Amazing Apple as it bobbed in the water.

It looked extra shiny after its bath.

"Next it will go to the conveyor belt to be sorted," said Abe. "Follow me!"

The conveyor belt was loaded with wet apples.

Workers with white hats and coats stood by the belt.

They grabbed and tossed and grabbed and tossed.

"If they see a bad apple, they remove it," Abe explained.

That would be a tough job, I decided.

They all just looked like nice, happy apples to me.

"All these apples are making me hungry!" Coco said. "Can we eat soon, Ms. Diz?"

"We're almost done with our tour, Coco," said Ms. Diz.

Suddenly the Amazing Apple appeared on the conveyor belt.

"There it is again!" I yelled.

Abe pointed to the Amazing Apple and asked a worker to grab it.

The worker tossed it to Abe. Abe tossed it to Wyatt.

Wyatt looked at the apple. He didn't seem that thrilled about having it back.

"It's all yours," Abe said to Wyatt.

"Ready to eat."

Wyatt looked over at Coco. "Hey, Coco," he said, "you're so hungry. Why don't you eat it?"

It was nice, seeing Wyatt be nice.

Unusual too.

Wyatt tossed the apple to Coco.

"Thank you, Wyatt," she said.

She took a great big, mouth-open-as-wide-as-possible bite of that beautiful Amazing Apple.

She chewed.

And chewed.

"Good, huh?" said Abe. "Isn't that the best apple you ever tasted?"

Coco made a face. "It tastes like . . . macaroni!"

She looked at the apple and gasped.

"EWWWWWWWWWW!" she screeched.

The apple dropped to the floor. "I ATE A WORM, MS. DIZ! I'M GOING TO DIE!"

"I think I'm going to faint," said Coco's mom.

If anybody had the right to faint, I figured it should be Coco.

"You'll be okay, young lady," Abe said. "It's just a little protein. Nothing to worry about."

"Wyatt," Ms. Diz said, "did you *know* that apple had a worm in it?"

"YOU POISONED ME!" Coco yelled at Wyatt.

"How could I know if it had a worm in it?" Wyatt asked.

He made an innocent don't-blame-me face.

I know that face. I've used it before.

Wyatt picked the apple up off the floor. "Besides, it's not like Coco ate the whole worm. Half of him's still in the apple."

"I don't feel so good," Coco moaned.

Everyone was looking at her. And you could tell they were all thinking, *I'M SO GLAD I'M NOT YOU RIGHT NOW.*

Even though Coco can be annoying sometimes, she didn't deserve to eat a worm.

Or even half a worm.

I pulled Hazel's magic ball out of my pocket.

"Magic ball," I said, "did Wyatt know there was a worm in that apple?"

I turned the ball over.

"'ABSOLUTELY, POSITIVELY YES!'" I read.

"Let me see that stupid ball!" Wyatt cried.

But before he could say anything else, someone fainted.

And it wasn't Coco's mom.

10

Boy-Flavored Applesauce

Coco lay on the floor.

"My baby's fainted!" Coco's mom cried.

Everyone crowded around to see what a fainted person looked like.

"Give her air!" Abe cried.

Wyatt looked at Coco. Then he looked at me.

"Let me see that ball," he repeated.

"No way!" I said. "It's my sister's."

Wyatt grabbed for the ball.

I turned and ran.

Nobody paid any attention. On account of Coco was busy fainting.

I zipped into the applesauce room to get away from Wyatt.

But he was right behind me.

A giant, loud machine was smushing apples.

Another one was stirring a huge tub of apple stuff.

It smelled sweet and cinnamony.

"Step away from the applesauce!" a loudspeaker voice yelled. "STEP AWAY FROM THE APPLESAUCE!"

I stopped running.

Wyatt tried to stop running too.

But he skidded on a slick spot.

Applesauce, probably.

He slid right into me.

Hazel's magic fortune-telling ball went flying.

Straight into the giant tub of applesauce.

It sank like a little red submarine.

"NO!" I screamed. "The magic ball!"

"STEP AWAY FROM THE APPLE-SAUCE!" the voice said again.

I couldn't jump in, could I?

Ms. Diz really wanted us to be on our best behavior.

I was pretty sure jumping into apple-sauce didn't count as best behavior.

On the other hand, I'd promised Hazel I would return her ball to her safe and sound.

Hazel was my little sister. She trusted me.

And she loved that ball.

There was only one thing I could do.

I leaped right into that giant tub.

The applesauce came up to my waist.

It was slimy. And oozy.

And tasty.

I reached down with both hands and felt the bottom.

But it was a very big tub.

And a very little ball.

I glared at Wyatt with mad eyes.

"You . . . you . . . you do NOT have a very winning personality!" I yelled.

I grabbed a handful of applesauce and flung it.

It landed—*splat!*—on Wyatt's face.

He scooped some off and tasted it.

"Not bad," he said.

"Bully breath," I muttered.

"Goo swimmer," he said.

"Ball stealer," I said.

"You have applesauce in your eyebrows," Wyatt said.

"You have applesauce in your nose hole," I said.

I smiled just a little.

So did he. Just a little.

"What's it like in there?" Wyatt asked.

"Gooey," I said.

"I can't believe you jumped in," Wyatt said in an admiring voice.

"Want some help?" he asked.

"Sure," I said.

Wyatt hopped in.

"WE HAVE A CODE RED IN THE APPLESAUCE ROOM! THERE ARE CHILDREN IN THE APPLESAUCE!" said the loudspeaker voice. "REPEAT: THERE ARE CHILDREN IN THE APPLESAUCE!"

We both looked for the ball.

I stuck my head all the way under the applesauce.

I couldn't see anything. But I could reach a little farther.

I felt something roundish and slippery-smooth.

There it was at last! The magic ball.

Safe and sound, but sticky.

When I came up for air, everyone was there.

Ms. Diz. The moms. The dads. Abe. The white-coated workers.

Even Coco.

Their mouths were open.

They stared and stared, but nobody said a word.

I guess we looked a little slimy.

"Do we still get our free applesauce?" I asked.

11

Good-Bye from Time-Out

So that's how I ended up going for my applesauce swim.

And landed here in time-out.

My hair was pretty sticky when I got home.

So was Hazel's magic fortune-telling ball.

I think maybe some applesauce got stuck inside of it.

Because now when you ask it a question, it only has one answer: "ASK AGAIN LATER."

Hazel was awfully nice about it, though.

When I said, "Can I borrow it again sometime?" Dad said, "Ask again later."

My whole family's visiting the orchard next weekend.

Wyatt and his family are coming too.

We are going to pick enough apples to pay for the applesauce we ruined when we swam in it.

Apparently, nobody wants Roscoe-and-Wyatt-flavored applesauce.

So they had to throw the whole batch out.

That means we have to pick seven whole baskets of apples.

Emma's coming with us to the orchard.

She says the only way we're going to get that many apples is with her help.

I think maybe she's right.

Ms. Diz says Emma is a good buddy.

I have to agree with her on that one.

She also said our class might go on another field trip someday.

But not for a long time.

I am crossing my fingers for a chocolate-candy factory.

Think of the oozy, gooey chocolate everywhere!

How could I possibly get into trouble at a place like that?

ASK AGAIN LATER

10 COMPETITIONS WITH MY BIG BROTHER I AM PRETTY SURE I COULD WIN

by Me, Roscoe Riley

1. Who can produce the loudest armpit fart?

2. Who is the fastest at tongue twisters?*

3. Who can get the biggest wad of bubble gum stuck in his hair when blowing bubbles?

4. Who can make the coolest ugly face?

5. Who can make the biggest cannonball splash at the pool?

*Just in case you want to try it, here's my favorite tongue twister (say this as fast as you can!): Toy boat toy boat toy boat toy boat toy boat toy boat

6. Who can eat the most corndogs at our Fourth of July picnic (without throwing up)?

7. Who is the cutest smiler in the family? (Grandma could judge this one because I am almost positive I am her favorite.)

8. Who knows the best joke?*

9. Who can make the most original LEGO construction? (Last week I made a three-headed frog on a bicycle, although so far nobody has guessed what he is.)

10. Who is the best brother on the planet? (Okay, okay . . . maybe this one should be a tie.)

*Also, here's my most favorite joke:

Question: Why did the chicken cross the playground?

Answer: To get to the other slide!

Here's a super-special sneak peek at my next adventure,

The first time I heard Emma's tapping shoes was during show-and-tell.

Ms. Diz, my teacher, lets us bring all kinds of weird stuff to share with the class.

She is a brand-new teacher, so she likes to experiment on us.

Once Dewan brought a ferret. Which is like a stretched-out guinea pig.

After that, Ms. Diz made up the No Show-and-Tells that Can Bite rule.

Maya brought her grandpa's artificial leg to another show-and-tell.

After that, Ms. Diz made up the No

Show-and-Tells Without Permission of the Owner rule.

The same day Emma brought her tap shoes to school, I brought something from my Noisy Stuff collection.

I always bring noisy stuff for show-and-tell.

I LOVE noise!

Weird noise.

Funny noise.

And of course, best of all, LOUD noise.

Here's what I've collected so far:

Noisy Thing	Noise It Makes
1. Birthday-party horn	HONK!
2. Whoopee cushion	PFFFT!
3. Toy fire engine	Whee-oo-whee-oo!
4. Bongo drums	Bum-ba-bum-ba-bum!
5. Junior Rock Star Electric Guitar	SCREEEECH!

6. Cowbell	DONG!
7. Oliver, my stuffed elephant	Elephant hello (hard to describe, but it sounds a lot like my grandpa when he blows his nose)

The newest addition to my Noisy Stuff collection is my Mr. Megaphone.

It looks like a giant ice cream cone made of plastic. When you talk into the mouth hole, it changes your voice so you sound like a megamonster.

A loud megamonster with a bad cold.

When it was my turn for show-and-tell, I yelled, "Take me to your leader, first graders of the Earth!" into the megaphone.

Half the class covered their ears.

The other half went "WHOA!"

"Roscoe, that's a fine addition to your Noisy Stuff collection," Ms. Diz said. "Thank you for sharing it."

"I can pass it around," I offered.

"Please, NO!" Ms. Diz said. "I mean, we have other people who want to share this morning. Speaking of things that make noise, Emma, you have something special to show us today, don't you?"

Emma held up two black shoes with metal tappers on the bottom.

"These are my tap shoes," she said. "They make noise when you step."

Shoes with built-in noise? I thought. *What will they think of next?*

And that's how it all began.

Katherine Applegate is a big fan of apples (especially when they show up in a pie). Maybe it's because she has an "apple" in her last name. When she was little, kids sometimes called her "Kay Pear-fence," but she has forgiven them. Mostly. Katherine lives in Chapel Hill, North Carolina, with two kids, one husband, many pets, but sadly no apple trees.

Welcome to Roscoe Riley's world

of mishaps, mistakes, and way cool misadventures!

From bestselling author Katherine Applegate

When his classmates can't sit still for a big performance, Roscoe takes matters into his own hands.

Roscoe decides to give Wyatt, the class bully, a taste of his own medicine.

Roscoe goes to extremes to win a big, shiny trophy—even if it means borrowing someone else's dog.

Despite being on his best behavior, Roscoe finds himself in a sticky situation while on his first school field trip.

A super-mega-gonzo new series!

HarperCollinsChildren'sBooks
www.harpercollinschildrens.com